Diane Broeckhoven   Noëlle Châtelet
Annette Pehnt   Alissa Walser

Painting in a Man´s World

Edited by Ingrid Pfeiffer

Four stories about
Berthe Morisot
Mary Cassatt
Eva Gonzalès
Marie Bracquemond

HATJE
CANTZ

Contents

Ingrid Pfeiffer

Four Women Artists, Four Styles, Four Stories of Success and Failure

Scarcely any other era in the modern age can be considered as crucial to the self-perception of women as the second half of the nineteenth century. For it was then, for the first time in history, that middle-class women began of their own accord to pursue a career outside the family—a career which would not only provide them with an income of their own, but would also enable them to pursue their personal interests and put their talents to productive use.

Although these four stories are fictional, they are based on the biographies of four real women, which, taken together, exemplify very well the fate of women artists in the early days of modernism. Anyone who studies women's art in the age of Impressionism will soon realize that it involves far more than just conventional art history, which views art in terms of recognized styles, modernity or innovativeness and looks at artists' groupings and manifestos. The history of these women artists is social history, too, inseparably bound up with the circumstances peculiar to women living in the days before universal suffrage and before there was such a thing as sexual equality.

The four painters who are the subject of this book—three of them French, one American—lived and worked mainly in Paris, which at that time was Europe's art capital. Paris in the days of the Second Empire under Napoleon III was where the most creative spirits in the country congregated, among them writers such as Charles Baudelaire, Stéphane Mallarmé, and Emile Zola and precursors of modernism in the visual arts such as Eugène Delacroix and Gustave Courbet. The city itself came to symbolize the new—from the building of splendid and expansive boulevards to the brisk pace of industrialization and the expansion of trade and commerce. World Expositions and modern street lighting spread the city's fame worldwide, making Paris synonymous with culture and modernity. Not by chance did so many American painters, one third of them women, come to study in Paris during the age of Impressionism.

Yet much of what Paris had to offer in the way of modernity was beyond the reach of women. Unlike their more famous fellow painters such as Monet, Manet, Degas, Renoir or Pissarro, Morisot, Cassatt, Gonzalès, and Bracquemond were not allowed to come and go as they pleased. Unmarried, middle-class women could leave the home only with an escort and if they cared about their reputation could not enter cafés and restaurants or visit the theater on their own. Their realm was the home, the garden, and the family—themes which were reflected for the first time in Impressionist art, including that painted by men. Especially important to these women artists was the Louvre, in which painters and sculptors copying old masters could meet and exchange views as professional equals and people of like mind.

Women painters and sculptors were also prevented from receiving the same training as their male counterparts, since the French Academy, the Ecole des Beaux-Arts, was closed to women right up until 1897. There had long been painting schools for women only, of course, and some well-known painters welcomed the presence of ladies in their painting classes—all the more so as they were often required to pay twice as much in fees! The Salon, that great annual art show featuring the works of some 3,000 artists, may have been open to women in principle—at least if the jury deemed their works to be worthy of inclusion—but the medals, prizes, and awards that were so crucial to an artist's success were almost always bestowed on men.

As many women belonging to the upper middle classes painted oils or watercolors or became accomplished musicians before they got married, the distinction between talented amateur and professional artist was for a long time blurred. Asserting oneself as an artist in defiance of society's straitjacketing required both determination and a readiness for self-sacrifice. That the four women artists selected for this exhibition represent not just four different styles and four different approaches to art, but also four very different biographies, each of which is in its own way typical, is symptomatic of this. Mary Cassatt, for example, chose not to marry so that she could devote herself exclusively to her art; Eva Gonzalès died at the age of thirty-four shortly after giving birth to her first child; Marie Bracquemond became so worn down by her jealously domineering husband, who regarded her as a rival, that in the interests of "family peace" she eventually abandoned painting altogether. Only Berthe Morisot had what, for that age, was the very rare good fortune to find a husband who encouraged her in her work and supported her exhibitions even after they got married and had a child.

Zola called on the artists of his age to depict "real life," and Morisot, Cassatt, Gonzalès, and Bracquemond took up this challenge in much the same way as did their male counterparts, by painting scenes of everyday life, portraits, still lifes, and landscapes. They often had their sisters sit for them, painted together with them or, like Morisot, painted their own husband and child in the garden. Each one of the four developed her own distinctive style, which was just as modern and unmistakable as is that of many of their male colleagues, who are much more famous today.

While countless women artists of the nineteenth century are scarcely known to us by name and those works of theirs that have survived in museum basements or private collections are still waiting to be discovered, Morisot, Cassatt, and Bracquemond, who regularly took part in the big Impressionist exhibitions, and Gonzalès, who like her teacher Manet was a member of the group's inner circle, achieved both recognition and success during their lifetime. This almost certainly has to do with the success of the Impressionist movement itself, for it was Impressionism that caused them to be seen and taken seriously by their contemporaries and contemporary art critics. Morisot, for example, came to be described as the most "impressionistic of the Impressionists," while Cassatt was praised for both her powerful, "manly" style, and her unsentimental portraits of mothers and children. Gonzalès was celebrated as a gifted protégé of Manet and an excellent pastel painter, while Bracquemond ranked among the *Grandes Dames* of Impressionism.

That the fame of the male Impressionists for a long time all but eclipsed that of their female counterparts has a lot to do with the fact that twentieth-century art history was to a large extent "invented" and written by men. After all, there is no objectivity in the reception of art

and here, as elsewhere, the truth lies in the eyes of the beholder. Not until the special circumstances under which women artists had to operate became a focus of critical attention in the 1980s did these women Impressionists return to the art historical field of vision. These days, however, they are represented in most general works on Impressionism and their paintings regularly fetch high prices at auctions and on the art market.
The four authors whose stories are published here have intuited their way into the lives of these four women painters, knowing that sometimes, there is more truth in fiction than in the retelling of a known biography. For of far more interest to us than pure facts is the psychology of these women, who after all belonged to the age which did most to shape the conditions under which we live today and which is actually much closer to us than we care to believe.

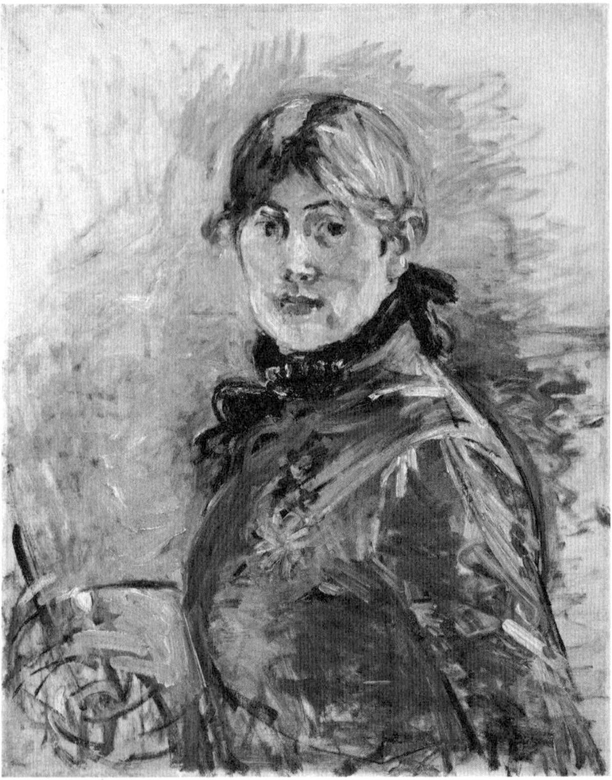

Berthe Morisot, *Self-Portrait,* 1885

Alissa Walser

Her Life, Not Her Picture

She never wanted to get married. She always finds out only later what she wanted. Three girls with braids, Yves, Edma, Berthe. Each one like a copy of the others. Their mother puts them in long dresses. With bows and ribbons. Colorful dolls. In the afternoons their father takes them to the trolley in the carriage. From the trolley the streets look bright and open. A horse on the tracks pulls them half way round Paris. It's Berthe's idea to draw the horse in its harness. The drawing teacher picks them up. He has a face that goes better with the carriage than with the trolley.

The sisters practice shading. Berthe forgets the horse. Diagonal lines and yet more diagonal lines, month after month. So many lines darken a picture. Yves gives up. Something normal, she says, something useful, sewing maybe, and later, when she grows up, get married?

Berthe starts a new page. Normal? she says. Normal!

She asks Edma to choose, painting or marriage.

Art or life. Who said that? Later!

Painting, Edma says. Painting is normal. Now they are a twosome.

Together they plead for a new teacher. Two females with a secret life, their mother calls them. Dreams forge bonds.

When Berthe dreams she sees pictures. Blossoming gardens and women in voluminous dresses, sitting, reading. The mother finds a new teacher. There is no shortage of teachers. In the Louvre the girls wear hats and copy old masters. They paint women who are naked. Talented daughters, the teacher tells the mother. So talented that it will end badly. The father builds a studio for the daughters in the garden. Their realm, he calls it. Our secret realm, the girls call it.

In the Louvre they meet friends. These lead like a lit fuse to new friends. Fantin, Claude, Georges, Puvis, Edouard, Edgar.

Young, curious, and full of ideas. Ideas are normal. Like Berthe and Edma.

She is, Berthe says to Edouard, fed up with the Louvre.

You mean the dust, Miss, not the pictures.

Or the pictures dusty-musty from within?

Like in the Salon?

Nice to be understood by a painter like Edouard.

In the evenings, when the men go to the café, the girls return to their realm. They stretch canvases or heat glue to soften it, what they are missing out on they don't miss.

Disguised as men, Berthe says to Edma, we could go there too.
Is anyone interested in heated debates?

Corot, the latest teacher, takes the girls to the Bois de Boulogne. Painting in the open air. Breathe deeply and forget everything that went before. A clean sheet.
The world consists of light, says Papa Corot.
They are sitting in little boats, trying to keep a steady hand while rocking.
A woman. She is leading her child by the hand up the three steps to a fountain. That's normal. In painter tempo. Red- and yellowish green-flecked trees in the autumn sun. Haze. In the distance a bell sounds, but not a death knell. Berthe sees everything, feels everything.
One step is missing from her picture. Be precise.
Precise? she says, looking into her teacher's face.
Painstaking, he says.
When he praises Edma, Berthe bends low over her picture. In the studio she hangs it on the wall.
Nothing remains of the mood in the park.
One can't simply scratch the color off normal things and paint over them.
Moments can't be repeated. They light up, and then they are gone. Counters of steps miss what's most important.
By evening the picture has been painted to death. Even an inadvertent murder is unpardonable.

A glance at Edma's work and she sees her path becoming longer in front of her. She sees herself counting steps into infinity.
Berthe's preference for everything that is hard to master. Water, women, meadows, passers-by at the beach, waves, glances, the sea. And the tones of watercolors, lucid and flowing. She dreams of masterpieces: oil paintings, bright and lucid, as if painted with water.
The watercolor itself determines who is a true master.
Water (most of the time), she thinks.
Normal life goes on.
Mother calls them to supper. The set table: sumptuous bouquets of flowers, and plates painted with oriental, long-tailed birds.
Her daughters should lack for nothing. Not food or drink, nor conversation with the painters of the city. One evening a week: Tuesdays. Names like Puvis, Emile, Claude, Gustave, Pierre, Edgar, Edouard. The latter with his whole family.
The sisters wander through the house in muslin dresses like rustling blossoms. The cook lights a fire. A fire of color like a color of fire. Edma's dress shimmers like the inside of a shell.
Berthe tries to note all the tones of white. Noting something for oneself is like the white of the canvas. And how quick real life is. If Edma is not already sitting next to Edouard, Berthe will sit down beside him.

Edouard's parents remind Berthe of her own. This mixture of elegant joie de vivre. but rather joie de vivre than elegance. Does she radiate that herself?
At table everyone talks cheerfully to each other and all at once. Every sound a brush stroke, a perfect painting. What's new. Pierre and Puvis have been accepted by the Salon, Edgar was refused.
Can one take the jury seriously?
Better to start something of one's own.
An art dealer wants to buy more than twenty of Edouard's works. Edouard is becoming famous. Will he be rich too? Berthe's paintings and money are like water and oil. Berthe knows when mother begins talking about money, she'll end up with marriage. In defense, Berthe lays sentences out ready as sharp as her sharpened pencils.
You are like all of us, her mother says, talented. But we are without the energy to climb the ladder. That's how we are and that's how we'll remain.
If Berthe has learned one thing, it's this: Nothing remains as it is.
In response to the question, how and from what she plans to live alone, she sharpens her pencils.
She watches the maid clear the table, the newspapers with the art reviews, the dregs in the glasses. The "good night" at the end of the silence, or the meaningful silence at the end of a conversation about business and the lack of energy to climb ladders.

But with Berthe, her mother says, it's like with her work, she receives many compliments but no one is seriously interested in her.
She asks her whether she doesn't want to lead a normal life.
Normal? Berthe leads her mother by the hand to her studio. You look so unhappy when you paint, her mother says softly, and then such pretty pictures emerge.

Edouard always talks loudly and always clearly: you can only paint the way you paint, isn't that so? And then when you have to fight your way into the Salon, you have to be both oil and water.
Berthe whispers to Edma, except for their opinions Edouard's family is the mirror image of our family. But instead of three sisters three brothers look out from the mirror. Three hairy faces: Edouard, Eugène, Gustave. Look at their beards, Berthe says, and shudders.
Edouard lets them show him their most recent work. Berthe doesn't listen when he praises Edma's hair-thin stroke. She starts listening again when he says to her: You, you have everything that's required. You just have to *want*.
Berthe wants to want. The constant fear that her wanting is greater than her ability. She takes it amiss that he is laughing.
He asks whether she will sit for him.

Yes, I will.
When the guests have left and the cook is dumping the cinders on the ash heap, Edma stands before Berthe with a face like a Hieronymus Bosch: She asks how she finds Edouard's wife?
A little fat, Berthe says, but she plays the piano well.
Why did Berthe say yes? Edma wants to know.
Does Berthe think Edouard is interested in her pictures.
He's really interested in her.
Berthe senses Edma's envy.
Anyway, Berthe says quickly, Eugène paints too.
What's that supposed to mean, Edma runs out, into the light.

Berthe's time, the time of the railways. Black like the black of cadmium-red, phthalo-green and -blue. And smudged a little.
Like a painting by Turner. So in the summer Berthe and Edma travel to the sea.
In gigantic clouds of steam. Zinc-white and titanically airy.
All attempts to explore lead to the beach. Where Edouard's family is vacationing too. Edouard's mother with an umbrella on a blanket in the sand.
Edma and Berthe in bathing costumes. The latest Paris fashion. Berthe, ready to swim, Edma not to be induced into the water. Edouard's mother, looking at Edma, says:

Mademoiselle Edma's great triumph is her bathing costume.
In search of motifs they draw a footprint, a line that fills with water, across the shore. Endlessly along the sea, the great horizon that divides everything. A landscape with sea is better to paint, Edma says. Things are differentiated so clearly. Like above and below. Not-blue and not-yellow. And the people on the quay, and the ships, Sunday normality.
Too much commotion, Edma protests, she suggests going inland a ways.
Berthe knows her sister means the clusters of children who gather behind the painters, their glances wedged between the world and the picture, and their comments! You have to learn to bear it.
When Edma resists, Berthe speaks the magic word that dispels every disagreement between the sisters: Edouard.
His pictures are models, about that they agree.
They are wild, Berthe says, unripe fruit. And how he captures a face.
And every dot, Edma says, is alive, is now, this moment. Like you or me.

Time doesn't stand still. Fall takes them back to Paris. The sisters submit the fruits of their labor to the Salon. They are accepted. But her joy at her success evaporates when Berthe discovers in the reviews that she is being compared to Papa Corot. Don't her pictures speak for themselves? Why does the world always need a father for everything? Is she herself perhaps an illusion, does she not really exist?

Back in her realm Berthe burns nearly all the work she has done.

She stands in the garden and gazes into the fire. She knows what it feels like to murder something. This time deliberately.

She turns around and sees a man running from the studio through the garden to the house. German uniform, gray.

But no, she is deceiving herself. She's got the wrong time.

One Tuesday afternoon Berthe receives Edouard. She has dressed up: a black outfit, a black hat. She has pinned the posy of violets to her dress. She sits for him till evening.

How do you paint time? How do you paint the previous glance? A second of time?

She admires Edouard. Without preparing a sketch he paints directly in oils. She studies Edouard's broad head, his frizzy beard, hair, the hair of his beard. A transparency behind which something is going on that simply won't conceal itself.

How do you capture something that never stops moving? Should you capture it at all? Isn't it better to paint something as it vanishes?
When Berthe tries to capture something she feels too slow.
And all the rules make her even slower.
At table Edma was quicker again. Berthe sits down beside Eugène. Eugène mentions a trip. Plans to paint and write. Berthe pricks up her ears.
The cook serves pheasant, perhaps boeuf bourgignon as well. In Turkey they nearly always eat lamb. On the ornate oriental menus: only lamb. Constantinople, the metropolis of the sheep-eaters. Beside Eugène she feels ignorant, but by no means hopelessly so. She acquires a book by Darwin. The world, nothing but a competition wherever you look? Darwin makes her sad.
Compared to his brother, Eugène is slender, and his beard seems impenetrable. An undergrowth behind which he hides himself. No one can hide himself unless he's a child. A penny for your thoughts, Eugène often says when she looks at him. She doesn't betray herself. The discrepancy between his appearance and how directly he talks about something. Berthe doesn't know whether she can really think the beard away. It creates space for the face. Without the beard it is too small. A small picture.

But the great difference—between Eugène and Edouard: What a palette of colors she would need in order to distinguish between the two.
After dessert back to the new picture in the studio.
Edouard follows her. She is startled when he reaches for a brush.
It's perfect, she says. Edouard looks at her questioningly.
He makes a few strokes on the canvas. She holds her breath. As if she could protect the picture from his eagerness.
She breathes a sigh of relief when he stops.
Well? he says.
Still perfect, she says, and watches him wash the brush in soapy water.
He wants to know if she knows that she is a beautiful and talented woman.
She says, as a painter he shouldn't use the word "beautiful" so carelessly.
He asks her whether she has thought about marrying?
Berthe rolls her eyes. Doesn't he know that marrying is a synonym for no-longer-being-allowed-to-paint.
That, he says, depends on whom one marries.
She laughs. She asks how one can know that.
She is beautiful and clever, he says. Breathtaking.
He is repeating himself, she tells him and asks whether this is going to become a double portrait of her
And she is obstinate, too, he continues.

She waits.
She is perfect for his brother, he says. Eugène.
She looks away abruptly, as if the sound of the name had flung her out of the picture. No, he wasn't repeating himself.
She tells him she suspects Eugène has sent his brother to her.
No, Edouard says, Eugène would never allow that.
That would make him appealing, she says, giving Edouard a rag and, while he is drying his hands, leaves the room. He never repeats himself, not in a single picture.

Eventually it happens: Edma topples out of the frame. She marries a naval officer. Berthe suppresses her questions and comments. Like a lump in her throat, as if she had swallowed turpentine. She flees to her realm. Who is she supposed to quarrel with now? She wants to talk about subjects for paintings. But a married sister is not a subject if you are not married yourself.

Letters from Edma: she longs for the secret life, she writes. For the smell of oil paints, just for five minutes. Berthe weeps. She gathers a bouquet of sunflowers, poppies, and meadow flowers. Hardly has she picked up her brush when flower petals fall on the table.
Alone, she writes, you become sad whatever anyone says or does, a woman needs tenderness. A woman can't

withdraw into herself. Be glad you have a husband who loves you, you alone. Here in the studio everything keeps repeating itself: standing around and guessing what one wants, and knowing what one is capable of—that too is pointless.
It's so comforting to comfort Edma.
Edma answers promptly in a few words: she is pregnant.
Berthe immediately has a belly in her head: vividly vaulted.
She paints the pregnant woman, and it's as if she were painting herself. A picture of the world that matches her. A self-portrait of the world.
She herself in another life. But for her it is a life that goes on. In winter their father dies.

In summer she goes with mother and Edouard's family to Normandy.
By the sea with Eugène: painting and swimming.
Eugène reads the newspapers, all the Paris and London ones, every day.
Berthe wants to swim every day. And paint. Best to do both together. Illuminate and be illuminated.
When he takes her back to the hotel, Eugène sometimes sounds as if the Prince of Wales, the Duc de Mouchy, were his old acquaintances.
And he says things like: It's so sad to court the moon. The sun burns itself trying. He would gladly pay court to

her, he says, for a thousand years if he could see her at least once a week. She needn't begin reading Voltaire for his sake, it was enough that she could paint, and besides she had read Darwin. Anyway, he said, he certainly doesn't make you sad; indeed, Darwin is women's reading, absolutely.

Berthe doesn't understand this man. That pleases her. When he's with her she feels she's a painter. She feels his enthusiasm, for her, for her pictures. He is clever, more cultured than his brother. And what he can't do as well as his brother, she can do: she can paint.

They sit on the beach and sketch boats being built.

A windy day. The wind drives dark clouds across the canvas. And strands of hair like sea salt from Berthe's hairdo. Eugène only has eyes for Berthe's picture. It has what a picture needs. She should take it with her to Paris, he says Paris needs good pictures. There are so many bad ones. Of cows where you don't know where the head is and where the tail. Eugène prophesies her success. Believe me, I know, he says when Berthe doubts. Then he turns to look at her—her hair bleached by the sun, tousled by the wind. She sees his horror.

Let's go, he says turning away, before you dissolve.

When she has her hair under control he is cheerful.

He shows her his watercolor. A penny for your thoughts, he tries to read her, looking for praise. She does him the favor and falls into raptures. Unreserved raptures.

Eugène puts his arm around her. A word, a Turkish word: *kuzum*, "my little lamb." In the language of the sheep-eaters you can't call a woman anything more appetizing. Returning to his mother tongue, he says that since seeing Berthe in the outfit that he would have to call Mademoiselle Edma's triumph, he has been carried away. She, his goddess, he wants to honor her as befits a goddess.
She would not have expected so much emotion from an intellectual.

In the fall they announce their engagement.
Berthe works. They marry in December. She in a dark dress, simple, in mourning. This is her life, not her picture.

Friends come to visit. On Thursdays. Pierre-Auguste, Edouard, Claude, Emile, Edgar, Stéphane or whatever their names are.
Berthe has remarkable dishes served: rice à la mexicane. Eugène looks everywhere for a position but finds none. She paints him. She draws him. Oil and water. When he doesn't happen to be reading the newspaper or writing, he helps her stretch canvases and ground them. He measures pictures and chooses frames. He tells her how good the pictures are. He discusses subjects. Edma is her subject, whom she no longer misses. He sits for her. He

hangs her pictures on the wall. Berthe produces painting after painting, she has never produced so much. And at the same time she tries to become pregnant. Too late. She was always too slow. And life gets quicker and quicker.
In April she exhibits with other painters in a photographer's studio.
Like a cat running over the keys of a piano, or like an ape that has got hold of a box of paints, is the verdict of one critic about the exhibition. Another calls the painters mentally disturbed.
Edouard wants to challenge the critic to a duel. Berthe forbids him to.
Aren't we all apes, before we become ourselves?

In the fall her mother dies.
Berthe has a girl. She would rather have had a boy.
First of all, the baby looks like a boy anyway, and second, a boy could pass on the famous name. And besides: doesn't the whole world, women and men alike, love the masculine gender?
She hasn't bothered looking for subjects for a long time. She is surrounded by subjects. Julie and Julie and Julie. Julie at her nurse's breast. Berthe herself never nursed her: everyone does their best. Julie with a doll in the armchair, in the garden with flowers. Julie with Eugène. Julie with a fiddle. Whatever she does, Julie is always

Julie. Berthe catches herself wanting to capture this face, unconditionally. Unconditionally, how is that to be done, in painting? She wants every one of Julie's glances to be art. Art is the child. Life goes on.

Berthe Morisot (1841–1895)

1841	Berthe Morisot is born in Bourges on January 14, the third of four children. Her father is a civil servant.
1852	The Morisots move to Paris.
1855	The three sisters Yves, Edma, and Berthe are given private drawing and painting lessons by Geoffroy-Alphonse Chocarne, and later by Joseph Guichard.
1858	Morisot makes her first copies of old masters at the Louvre, where she meets Félix Bracquemond and Henri Fantin-Latour.
1860	She meets Camille Corot who becomes a friend of the family.
1864	Her father has an atelier built in the garden for Berthe and her sister Edma. She makes her debut with two landscapes at the Salon de Paris.
1865–73	Morisot exhibits regularly at the Salon.
1868	Morisot meets Edouard Manet. They frequently work together and influence one another. The Morisots' and Manets' weekly soirées are attended by artists and writers such as Charles Baudelaire, Emile Zola, and Edgar Degas.
From 1874	Morisot helps to organize and takes part in all the Impressionists' group exhibitions

	(except that in 1879). She marries Eugène Manet, Edouard's younger brother.
1875	Morisot's works fetch the highest prices at an auction at the Hôtel Drouot with Monet, Sisley, and Renoir
1878	Birth of her daughter Julie
1879	The friendship between Berthe Morisot and Mary Cassatt deepens.
1883/84	Morisot takes charge of a memorial exhibition for Edouard Manet at the Ecole des Beaux-Arts and later of sales of his works, too.
1886	Exhibition of her own works at the Galerie Durand-Ruel in New York
1892	First solo exhibition at the Galerie Boussod, Valadon & Cie. in Paris. Morisot's husband Eugène Manet dies on April 13. Stéphane Mallarmé is named Julie's guardian.
1894	First purchase of Morisot's works for the Musée du Luxembourg
1895	Berthe Morisot dies on March 2.
1896	Her friends Mallarmé, Degas, Monet, and Renoir organize a large memorial exhibition at the Galerie Durand-Ruel.

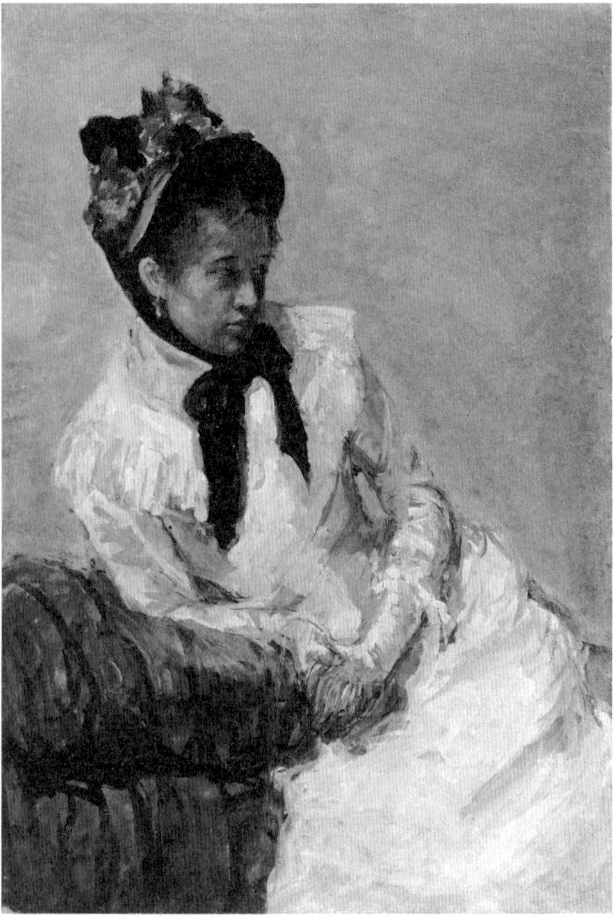

Mary Cassatt, *Self-Portrait*, 1878

Diane Broeckhoven

Clair-obscur

May 25, 1926

In my dream I took flight, like a bird setting course for the sun, but at the same time gravity pulled me heavy-handedly earthwards. The bang echoed through my fragile spine. I awoke with a start and my eyes shot open. The bedroom was shrouded in pitch-black darkness. But through the window with the open curtain—a ribbon of light in the corner of my eye—I could see that the darkness outside was already disintegrating into shadowy patches. A creamy, almost full moon hung breathlessly between the branches. The birds here* with their shrill cries that every morning reminded me I wasn't in Paris were deathly silent. The depths of night had passed and dawn was about to break.

In that hour between sleeping and waking, as nightfall lifts and vague colors reveal themselves, I had fallen out

* In Beaufresne, eighty kilometers north-west of Paris.

of bed. It seems to be one of the infirmities of my old age. As stiff as my body has become during the day, so slackly and without constraint it behaves at night. When sleep does its work on me, my taut muscles relax and I become young again. Sometimes in my dreams I'm standing there in a trance, mixing colors, painting. I'm swimming, flying. Floating in the water, in the air. I'm galloping through fields on my horse again. I fall. At a certain point I always fall out of my own décor again.

Like an upturned cockchafer, its tiny legs churning hopelessly in the air, I lay there on the floor. I was unable to roll onto my side and, from that position, perhaps sitting on my knees, try to grab the edge of the bed. The thought alone of this succession of physical activities tired me so much that the life seemed to ebb out of all my limbs. The sharp pain in my spine, worn out from standing erect at my easel for hours on end, imprisoned me within myself. I abandoned any attempt to try to stand up on my own.

I pricked my ears to hear if there were any signs of life in the house. But apart from my own wheezy breath, there was only the whispering silence. I desperately hoped that Mathilde, my vigilant Mathilde* who slept downstairs, had registered the tremor caused by my fall in her subconscious, and would quickly throw a dressing-gown over her nightclothes and come and rescue me from my distressing situation. Perhaps she rolled over again and dreamt of an earthquake as I had of my flight to the sun on languorous wings. A person has a right to his own dreams. It remained silent. I called her name three times, but my voice was so weak it caused only a slight ripple in the darkness. The sound of footsteps on the stairs failed to materialize.

My nightdress had crept up above my bony knees. I strained to lift my head a few centimeters and glimpsed the lead-white stripe of my skinny legs against the dark floor. I shivered—from the cold and the horror.

My eyes, which have been damaged by diabetes, can still distinguish light from dark. During the day, when the sunlight is at its brightest, I can sometimes make out the colors of the chrysanthemums and the roses in the flowerbeds. Then I drink in the tawny tea colors, the imperious magenta, the dark-red shades of old burgundy and blood. Then I stroke the velvet petals, aware of how

* Mathilde Valet, Mary Cassatt's faithful housekeeper from 1882.

the touching sharpens my memories. After painting, gardening was something I could put my heart into. Rooting about in the earth healed my soul. Like my paintings, the flowers were my creations, my children whom I had to let go yet who are the comfort of my old age.

Years ago I resigned myself to the blindness, which occurs in varying waves of intensity. And to the black-rimmed bottle-bottomed glasses that weigh so heavily on the ridge of my nose. But seeing my emaciated body stretched out across the floor at this nocturnal hour like a streak of chalk shocked me. I was merely a shadow of myself. Not even a blueprint suggestive of potential and a future, only the shadowy, pale remnant of the person I had once been.

Most of all I wanted to die, however humiliating my present circumstances were. An old woman lying helplessly on her back, like the young man transformed into an insect in the story by the Jewish writer who caused such a stir—her nightdress rolled up, her bare legs a roadmap of blue veins ... Mathilde, who has known me in all my glory and all my vulnerable nakedness, would undoubtedly treat my body, now frozen alabaster-white, with respect. She would only notify Louie* and any other remaining members of my family after she had restored my dignity. That thought calmed me.

As I lay there longing for deliverance, I heard the first cry of a bird. A blackbird. The shrill sound shot through the air like a missile, announcing the new day. My hand flew automatically to my good ear, the right one, and registered that my batiste night-cap had slipped backwards during the fall. I straightened it with trembling fingers, tucked my thin hair under the edges and tied the ribbons under my chin again. I had to laugh at my own folly, at this misplaced vanity in the face of death. The darkness in the room had faded to a bluish-grey. I could see the contours of the linen cupboard, and the pastel-colored porcelain of the water jug lit up on the chest of drawers. My eye suddenly caught on the white bedspread folded on the chair next to my bed, one corner within reach of my hand. As I touched the handwork, firm and soft at the same time, tears welled into my eyes. I saw my beloved eldest sister Lydia as clear as day before me in the garden at Marly, where she crocheted patches with endless patience that she later sewed to-

* Louie, the pet name for the American Louisine Havermeyer.

gether. The image of her moving hands, of the thread crawling across her skirt like a wriggling worm, the crochet hook dancing rhythmically between the loops: all her sisterly love was woven into that spread. I pulled it off the chair with my last ounce of strength. Luck was with me: the spread unfolded slightly and I was able to pull it over me without much trouble. My feet were still uncovered, luminous like pale starfish.

Yet a salutary warmth flowed in through the hundreds of little holes in the crochet pattern and before long brought my chilled body back to life somewhat. As the growing numbers of birds emitted an imbroglio of sounds, the many shades of dark green in the tree crowns stood out against the yellow-grey firmament. The moon had been extinguished. If the Grim Reaper were to steal into my room now with his black hood obscuring his head, I might send him away. I longed for life again, though just a few shades of darkness earlier I had invoked death.

Mathilde would be awake soon. She would dress herself, put on her white apron and make strong morning tea for me with herbs from the garden. She would pour a fresh infusion of eyebright into the little white bowl and lay out clean compresses, with which she dabbed my eyes every day. Were those her steady footsteps I heard on the stairs? It must be my hope and my imagination that made the stairs creak—because nothing happened. The bedroom door remained closed.

I was always independent during my working life. I thoroughly enjoyed my own company, though at times it was considered selfish. Now, like a helpless child, I was longing for a mother figure to nurture and comfort me. Mathilde! She's the one to whom I entrust myself in the perilous days of my old age. She's the only person who has always tacitly understood me, who respected my need to work without interruption, who adapted herself to my free spirit. Her combination of servile and dominant qualities make her unique. We each had our own domestic plots. She even managed to convert my guests, accustomed to generous portions of meat on their plates, to vegetarian dinners. On orders from me, without protest. At the end of the meal she served fresh mint tea with a dash of valerian. The unusual *digestif* was consumed, baby fingers daintily raised. One guest later admitted that the nightcap had enhanced his sleep and his digestion. But most just laughed or gossiped about my unconventional lifestyle.

If there had ever been a man in my life with the same selflessness as Mathilde, I might have said yes. To my good friend James Stillman's* proposal I said no. Unhesitatingly, in both French and English. Yet I was very fond of him. There was a form of love between us, but not the kind of love for which you relinquish everything. James knew that art and money had a lot to do with each other. He bought twenty-four of my canvases. This flattered me of course but at the same time it fuelled my doubts. Was it the woman Mary he loved or the prestige of the painter? I never managed to find out. James was a lovable man-of-principle. I often wondered why someone with these qualities, a father of three, would wish to divorce. Who could guarantee he wouldn't do the same to me? I would have found it humiliating.

I continued to lie frozen under the spread as a diffuse light seeped into the room. I pushed one corner of the heavy fabric between my neck and the floor so as to lie more comfortably. For a moment I considered a second attempt to stand up. But the nagging pain in my back

* James Stillmann (1850–1918), an American banker who settled permanently in Paris in 1909, was a close friend of Mary Cassatt.

stopped me and I knew for certain that my ice-cold feet would no longer be able to support me. Mathilde could appear any moment now. She had to. She would help me up, bring me back to life. I was tired, so tired.

James's face loomed up crystal-clear behind my half-closed eyelids. It was fortunate that our friendship had reached its peak during our best years. Of course I felt sad when he died, but not so terrified and orphaned as when my dear mother passed away. I had difficulty reconciling myself to her death. For years I longed for a sign from her. I even attended spiritual séances in Paris at which I begged for a signal from the other side. It never came. Now that I'm ready for the big journey myself, I no longer seek it. I'm convinced I'll see all my loved ones again before long in a place far more beautiful than Beaufresne.

Degas* too left us some ten years ago. His tender yet cruel face loomed up in my mind's eye. My soft-hearted, stubborn friend Degas, whom I always suspected—deep in his heart—of being a misogynist. How could I have learned to love him without despising myself? Yet I did,

* Edgar Degas was also a close friend of Mary Cassatt and many saw them as lovers.

so deeply that it hurt. The suffering and scars were the proof of real love, I thought at the time. Degas was my blood brother. His artist's soul a branch of my own—or the other way around. My free spirit is reflected in my eyes and speaks proudly in my posture (though it is bent) in the portrait he made of me.* He is one of the few people who understood me, who didn't try to change me. He gave me a puppy once, lively and warm, a poor substitute for what he couldn't give me himself. It was as if the scent of that playful creature enveloped me under the spread.

This memory of Degas—too unreliable and restless to commit himself—was so intense it was almost as though he were standing in front of me. Again I could hear our good-natured squabbles, which often developed into heated rows with words as sharp as daggers. I saw us walking through the Louvre again, outdoing each other with our knowledge of the Masters. We were as different as night and day, yet at the same time as attuned to each other as the instruments of an orchestra. The brass and the strings. Is it nothing more than a coincidence that

* Between 1880 and 1884, Degas made a portrait of the then roughly forty-year-old Mary Cassatt.

two people who live with and through their senses become virtually blind at the end of their lives? First him, then me. Degas began sculpting when his eyes failed him. It was as if he himself were sculpted from granite or marble when he tackled the lumps of stone. Those were the moments I loved him most. I never told him this but with the sensitivity of someone who is losing his sight, he must have known.

Suddenly I smell the combination of paint, turpentine, and tobacco again. His manly scent, which belonged to my adolescent years and held such promise. A wave of warm excitement passed through my old body. Exhausted, I fell asleep, accompanied by a vague sense of shame.

I floated into a dream that carried me to the Nile. The trip with my brother Gardner and his family—which took us via Munich, Vienna, Budapest, Sofia, and Constantinople to Egypt*—has become a turning point in

* In late 1910 Mary Cassatt took a cruise on the Nile together with her brother Gardner (Gard), his wife, and their two daughters. The months of being away from home, the impossibility of working, and the lack of privacy resulted in a depression. Shortly after their return home in 1911, Gard died quite unexpectedly, which exacerbated her condition.

my life. How strange it was to be away from home for so long, unable to touch paint or brushes for months, apart from the box of watercolors I had taken with me. How confronting it was to have Gard's daughters around me all day long. Ellen Mary and Eugenia, the spitting image of their mother Jennie in their facial features, a reflection of their father in their cautious behavior. Never did I feel the absence of children of my own more poignantly than when I observed these girls in the phase between child and woman. I felt an emptiness more powerful and deeper than any I had ever felt when painting all my portraits of mothers and children. I had felt tender towards those mostly unknown children, but nothing more than that. The voices of my nieces aroused in me the longing for an extension of myself.

The dying sound of an agitated dog's barking awoke me. My hands had settled nostalgically on my belly. The bright daylight now cutting through the foliage in golden beams couldn't prevent me from feeling the same deep sadness that had taken possession of me after that journey. Gard had fallen seriously ill en route and died within a few months of our return. No matter how much Jennie and the girls needed my support, it was as if the loss of my brother destroyed my last resistance. The diabetes and rheumatism must have been gnawing away at the foundations of my being for months already. I sank into a deep depression. After the glory of fame, I landed in the hell of indifference. The light of my life went out and a fearful darkness extended farther than the eye could see. I lost weight until I was just skin and bones, and the doctors prescribed strict bed rest and seclusion. My thirst for independence mutated into an indescribable loneliness. During my sleepless nights I was visited by demons, and during the daytime it was as if my hands were shackled. My inner source had run dry. I could no longer paint. But a life without painting was no life.

I have always believed people are capable of healing themselves. And step by step this happened. First my spirit and soul, then—reluctantly—my body. To the outside world, the fact that I was standing in front of my easel again represented the ultimate proof of my recovery. "Start working again, madame, if only for ten minutes a day," my private physician admonished me. Even today, fifteen years later, his words make me sneer. Ten minutes a day! A painting isn't a piece of embroidery. Art requires a huge physical and mental effort. Whoever reduces art to a pastime for wiling away the hours is an amateur.

Louie and Mathilde saved me in those days—Louie through her letters and understanding, my faithful maid through her silent presence and devotion.

"Here, I say!"

Was that Mathilde I heard giving orders outside, interspersed with a nervous dog's barking? The sunlight eagerly found its way through the trees, sketching moving patches of light on the floor. My heart throbbed in my throat. It was unmistakably her voice downstairs at the kitchen door. She was awake. It wouldn't be long now. There was another sharp bark, then it was silent, an interminable silence. My throat and chest were covered with beads of perspiration while my feet were blocks of ice.

Then, at last, the sound of her footsteps on the stairs, coming up, closer by the minute. A stifled cough, a polite knock on the door, the vague apparition in the dark door-frame.

"Oh, Madame!"

My ministering angel. Always calm, never carried away by emotions. She quietly put the tray with the herbal tea, the white bowl, and the eye compresses on the little table and knelt down next to me.

"Oh, Madame," she repeated. Throwing off the spread, she carefully touched my body, establishing that there were probably no broken bones. It was only when her warm hands beneficently landed on my ice-cold feet that the tears started streaming down my cheeks.

"If it weren't for you, Mathilde …," I sighed.

"… then you would have had someone else!" she replied, soberly, rubbing my foot soles warm.

Firmly yet with infinite tenderness, she helped me to sit up. I was dizzy but she supported my back as if I were a baby, to ensure that I didn't topple over. Then she ordered me to put my arms around her neck and pulled me to my feet. My bones cracked quietly as she eased me backwards—one mouse step at a time—towards the edge of the bed. For a brief moment it was as though we were dancing together.

"Are you lying comfortably?" she asked, after I was stretched out on the bed again and she had fluffed up the pillows behind my shoulders.

"Like on a cloud," I replied.

She passed me the cup of tea. The fresh scent of the lemon balm and peppermint emboldened me. I drank a few sips and felt life embrace me again.

Mathilde folded the crocheted spread and lingered until sleep overwhelmed me again. "The dog escaped this morning," she chuckled. "He was chasing a rabbit. I just managed to stop him from catching it by throwing a broom at him."

She dribbled some St. John's oil on the palm of her hands and massaged my legs with careful, rhythmic movements. Then she covered me with the blankets again and gently instructed me to have a little nap.

"The day is young, Madame," she said, "it's only seven-thirty. I'll come for you in an hour and you can have your bath. I'll throw a sachet of fresh pine needles in the water, it will relax the muscles. Then you can have breakfast in front of the kitchen window. The strawberry jam is wonderful this year."

Tea, strawberry jam, pine needles in the bath ... Mathilde's love flowed into me, together with her words. My eyes closed, but a radiant white light shimmered through my eyelids that would remain with me for days and nights to come.

Less than three weeks later, on June 14, 1926, Mary Cassatt died peacefully in her sleep. Not long after, Mathilde Valet wrote in a letter to Louisine Havemeyer:

"Although she had many friends, no one in the world loved her more than you, Madame. And me. And she knew it."

Nancy Mowll Mathews, *Mary Cassatt: A Life.* (New Haven and London, 1994).

Mary Cassatt (1844–1926)

1844	Mary Cassatt is born in Pittsburgh, Pennsylvania. The family will later count among the most affluent industrialists in America.
1851–55	The Cassatts tour Europe.
1860	Cassatt enrolls at the Pennsylvania Academy of the Fine Arts.
1865	Cassatt moves to Paris.
1866	There, she attends Charles Chaplin's art classes for women. She also works from live models and copies works in the Louvre, as well as studying with Jean Léon Gérôme.
1867	The jury rejects the paintings she submits to the Salon de Paris.
1868	Makes her debut at the Salon, to which she will contribute regularly until 1876. Visits Barbizon.
1870	Owing to the Franco-Prussian War, she is obliged to return to Pennsylvania.
1871	Cassatt returns to Europe and visits London, Paris, Turin, and Parma together with Emily Sartain.
1872	She studies with Raimondi in Parma and copies two Correggios for the cathedral in Pittsburgh.
1877	Degas invites Cassatt to exhibit together with the Impressionists. She helps Louisine Elder Havemeyer with her first purchases of Impressionist art. These are the paintings that will form the rootstock of the Havemeyer Collection and later the Metropolitan Museum in New York.

1878	Cassatt's friendship with Camille Pissarro intensifies. One of her works is exhibited in the American Pavilion at the World Exposition in Paris.
1879	Cassatt forms a close friendship with Berthe Morisot and in the years following joins in the Impressionists' group exhibitions.
1881	Paul Durand-Ruel, the Parisian gallery owner, begins collecting her works and later exhibits them together with some by Morisot at his gallery in New York.
1882	Following a quarrel among the Impressionists, Cassatt asserts her loyalty to Degas by refusing to take part in the Impressionists' group show.
1890	Cassatt is very impressed by an exhibition of Japanese prints at the Ecole des Beaux-Arts and devotes more of her time to color prints.
1893	First major retrospective at the Galerie Durand-Ruel in Paris. Participation in the World's Columbian Exposition in Chicago.
1904	On December 31 Cassatt is made a member of the Legion of Honor.
1913	Cassatt takes part in the Armory Show in New York.
1925	Cassatt goes almost completely blind.
1926	Mary Cassatt dies on June 14 at her château in Beaufresne.

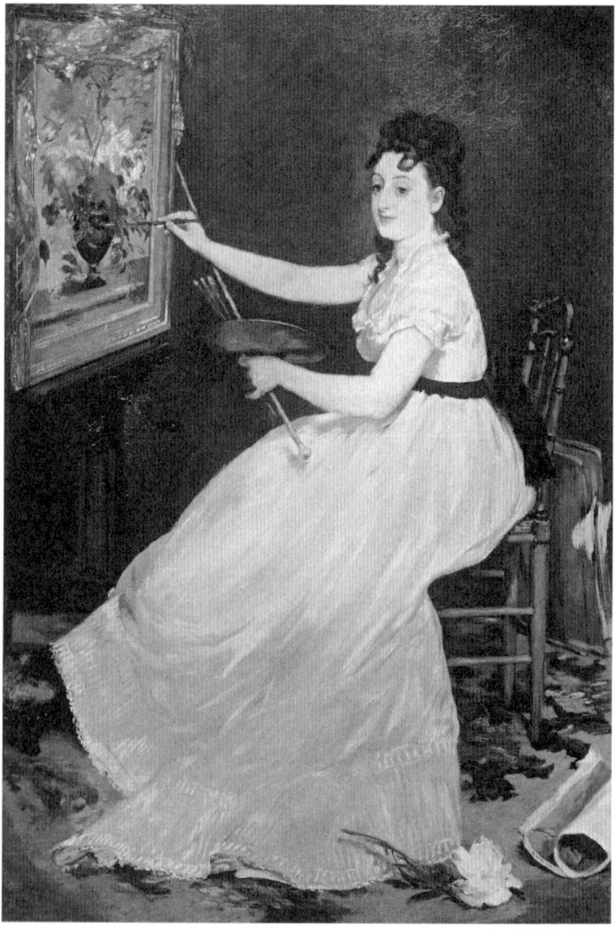

Edouard Manet, *Portrait of Eva Gonzalès*, 1870

Noëlle Châtelet

The Bridal Gown

February 2, 1879

With her gloved fingertips, Jeanne scratches at the door. Four times, faintly. This is the code. Their ritual. They call it "playing little mouse."

Eva isn't in the studio, but she can't have been gone long: in the air, along with the familiar, heady mix of oil, spirit, fish glue, and turpentine, floats the fragrance of a toilet water Jeanne knows only too well—because she uses it too.

She and Eva chose it together in the perfume shop on Rue Saint Georges, where the salesman was very much put out by these two beautiful young women determined to share something not meant to be shared: "Perfume, you understand, is something very personal, very intimate," he kept saying. But to no avail, for that was exactly what they wanted: to share the unshareable.

Jeanne smiles to herself. On the low table their plant is looking sickly. Eva has forgotten to water it again. No denying that her sister's recent marriage to Henri has upset their habits a little. Even so, it's clear that something's in the air.

To the left of the window Eva has set up the easel at an angle, in its carefully chosen place. The drawers of pastels are wide open and the blending stumps, little rolls of blotting paper, are arranged in order of size, like the dry brushes. Jeanne's full bosom swells with emotion, a mingling of curiosity and impatience: a new pastel work in the offing is something very special. The sight of the bare canvas on the easel, its virginal whiteness seemingly waiting for the firm yet caressing fingers that will soon leave their mark. All this is so terribly moving. And what is more—

And what is more there is always the secret, irrepressible hope that her older sister, her godmother both in the eyes of God—since her baptism at Notre Dame de Lorette—and in the eyes of the Muses, will speak the words, always the same, that have filled her with pride for years now: "Jeanne, tell me? Would you like to pose for me today?"

There's a little water left in the copper watering can. Jeanne pours it on the wilted plant, which seems to revive at once. A simple gesture, but once again to be savored, calling up as it does the unforgettable memory of a plant exactly like this one, watered in the same meditative way by the young Odette in her delicately waisted organdie dress...so like Jeanne today.

Barely seven years ago.

That day, while Eva concentrated on catching Odette's exquisite pose, Jeanne, as often happened when she was not posing herself, was sitting on the red leather sofa, unobtrusively following the elegant, rustling dance of the hand over the canvas; just as the youthful Eva herself had once done in Manet's studio, when she was his pupil.

From time to time Eva would explain the choice of a color or the meaning of a pose. Had not her younger sister, who had her own gift for painting, become her pupil in a way?

"What do you think of the curve of the shoulder?"

"It's perfect," Jeanne replied. "You can really feel the fabric."

"I need to rework the hand holding the carafe, don't you think?"

"Maybe you do. And what about more contrast between the flesh tone of the wrist and the transparency of the glass?"

It was then that Eva spoke those amazing words. Words never heard before. An offer that even today still moved her intensely, almost to the point of making her blush with shy pleasure.

"Alright then, what about giving me a hand?"

Jeanne sees herself getting to her feet, her legs shaking, her mind a blank.

"I'd like you to rework the movements of the plant in front of the body. Make it come to life, as if it's actually drawn to Odette, you see what I mean?"

"Yes, yes, I see..."

Now it was Jeanne's turn to approach the canvas, to pull the pastel drawer towards her with its gamut of greens, while Eva lingered over the gleam of the carafe from which the water was now beginning to flow. And one by one Jeanne had turned the leaves of the plant towards Odette's neck, Odette's breast, Odette's waist, as if the plant were seeking to embrace her, thank her for the bounteousness of this lifegiving water, and for the beauty of her gesture.

This dance had lasted a long time. For a long time their hands had crossed and recrossed on the canvas, in harmony and without once colliding, each young woman lost in her work, each aspiring to perfection as they moved towards a mutual ecstasy, a bonding for all eternity.

Never, surely, had they been more sisters than on that day. So much so that, a few months later, at the Salon of 1872, *The Favorite Plant*, the pastel born of their pas de deux was exhibited under the name of Jeanne-Eva Gonzales.

Jeanne puts down the watering can. Lost in her memories, still quivering at the recollection of a scene endlessly relived, she has not heard her sister come up behind her. How long has she been there?

Eva knows how sensitive Jeanne is. And must have seen her sister's eyes moist with tears as she turned.

"Everything all right?"

"Fine." Jeanne, too, is surprised, for on Eva's arm is a voluminous white dress she recognizes instantly. The bridal gown.

"You haven't put it away?" asks Jeanne.

"No. I haven't put it away," replies Eva. "Not yet."

A long silence.

Eva has the adamant look of someone wanting the impossible. Only their eyes speak during this long silence. Eyes so understanding that words are often unnecessary.

And then Jeanne grasps what her sister wants of her; this sister undaunted by the impossible, this sister to whom you offer no resistance, as impetuous as Jeanne is cautious, as demanding as Jeanne is submissive.

Eva holds out the gown and the headdress she wore on her wedding day.

Jeanne is no longer herself. Someone seems to be acting in her place. She takes the dress as if receiving an offering, her eyes lowered almost reverently, but her soul in a state of panic.

She undresses behind the screen with a confused feeling of receiving an undeserved favor; but there comes too the needle-sharp pleasure of transgression, together with an uncertain intuition that she is making some terrible mistake.

"Ready?" Eva is impatient.

No, Jeanne isn't ready. Will she ever be?

How can you be ready to put on your sister's bridal gown, only a week after her wedding? The dress Eva was wearing when she was blessed at Henri's side in the sisters' very own church, Notre Dame de Lorette.

Behind the screen Jeanne is trying to dress, clumsily.

"I can't do it up!" she whimpers.

Consumed by the coming picture, Eva seems in high spirits.

She pulls her sister from her hiding place and helps her. True, Jeanne is shorter and has a slightly fuller figure, and the bodice calls for more of an effort. With each hook she gives a cry that makes them both laugh out loud.

At last the collar is fastened.

"And now—the headdress!"

Eva appears to be having fun, like a child playing with a doll. Lifting Jeanne's long, dark brown curls she fits the bridal crown into place. There, it's done.

Now she leads her sister behind the easel, in the subdued, slanting light of the gray Paris morning. The light she loves most of all.

"My little Jeanne, you're so beautiful as a bride," says Eva. All of sudden serious—pensive, even.

"Strange," she goes on, "It's as if I were seeing myself."

Jeanne does not reply. Too many conflicting thoughts. And too many images. Eva on Henri's arm, such jubilation in the ninth arrondissement city hall. Rose petals raining down on the newlyweds. And two days later, to the sound of wedding bells, it's raining rice on the square in front of the church. Lots of laughter at the banquet afterwards. Succulent meat. And the peas *à la Manet*, specially prepared from a recipe by the Master—one of the witnesses at the ceremony—make the bride blush vigorously.

But no bells this morning, no showers of roses, rice, and laughter, no peas *à la Manet*; and without them the wedding dress seems funereal.

Eva has set to work.

Jeanne usually delights in the time spent posing for her sister: the scratching of the pastels and stumps on the canvas, Eva's eyes flicking repeatedly back to her face and body. As one pastel is put down and another taken up, Jeanne enjoys guessing which detail Eva is working on. As if she, Jeanne, were both model and artist.

This is watchful abandon, trusting attentiveness. Yet another way of being sisters. Their mutual presence in the world. Their way of celebrating having been born of the same womb, and having the same destiny: a sharing of art. Like the toilet water? Like the toilet water. Whether the salesman on Rue Saint Georges likes it or not.

None of that this morning.

Jeanne is feeling neither abandon nor that precious trust. For the first time, if she dared... But she doesn't dare. Doesn't dare say that this portrait, in that dress...

that she doesn't have a right to... That it isn't right. And anyway, Eva isn't there any more. Jeanne knows another Eva is at the easel, painting a bride.

It isn't right. But which Eva should she tell?

And which Eva would reply?

Even so, she tries. She tries a question.

"Eva, why? Why are you painting this portrait of me in your wedding dress?"

Eva looks at her sister. Really looks at her.

"I don't know," she replies. "But I have to."

* * *

The door of the studio is ajar. Eva slips inside, without "playing little mouse." She's taken advantage of Henri's absence—an appointment with his father at the Literary Society—to spirit away the dress, which for the last few days has been on the sofa in the bedroom.

She had the idea for the picture before the wedding, the day of the last fitting: her mother and the dressmaker were putting the headdress in place and at that exact moment, in the cheval glass, she saw the reflection of Henri studying her from the corridor, not daring to come in, not daring to break into an intimate, sacred moment.

She could not say why, or how, her fiancé's gaze troubled and even upset her. So many elusive expressions in that one look. As if he were seeing someone else, another Eva. It was then, yes, because of the strangeness of that gaze and almost in spite of herself, that she had the vision. She saw Jeanne in this bridal costume. Jeanne, her sister, that other part of herself. Her model, her double, born of the same womb and with the same destiny: a sharing of art.

Jeanne is watering the drooping plant. Wearing her organdie dress she radiates the same grace as Odette that day when, together, they drew her in the sublime pose of *The Favorite Plant*.

Eva has never forgotten that moment, stolen from the gods, when the two of them captured this flash of pure femininity; and the way Jeanne, following her advice, breathed life into the plant; and above all the way their dance brought them together so irrevocably.

Jeanne turns. Was she thinking the same thing?

"Everything all right?"

"Fine." Jeanne is visibly surprised to see the dress on her sister's arm.

"You haven't put it away?" asks Jeanne.

"No. I haven't put it away," Eva replies. "Not yet."

A long silence.
Jeanne has the desperate look of someone not wanting to understand. Only their eyes speak during the long silence. And yet Jeanne has understood. She takes the dress and disappears behind the screen.
Eva is ill at ease. She knows all too well that she is asking a great deal of this younger sister, so upright and submissive, whom she loves with a mixture of fascination and exigency.
Is she asking the impossible?
Maybe. But isn't this precisely what unites them: this taste for the extreme they have shared, always and perhaps forever?
The idea makes Eva impatient.
"Ready?"
No reply.
The organdie dress is hanging over the screen, but there is no movement on the other side. Eva is angry with herself now, but it's too late. Too late to draw back, for she is driven by something she doesn't understand.
Something she can't yet put a name to, but which seems to be engraving itself into her destiny because of Henri's look reflected in the cheval glass—so indecipherable, so troubled.

"I can't do it up!" Jeanne whimpers.

Eva is suffering for her sister. She must help her now, help her cope with this impossible demand. A game? That's it, make a game out of all this strangeness. So she pulls her sister out of her hiding place and laughing helps her do up the bodice.

At last the collar is fastened.

"And now—the headdress!"

Eva plunges her hands into Jeanne's marvelous hair, the hair she has painted so often, working from dawn till dusk. Hair flowing free or drawn into a chignon. Now she tames these tresses that ripple like silken serpents, and imprisons them in the nuptial crown. There, it's done. Eva leads her sister behind the easel, in the subdued, slanting light of the gray Paris morning. The light she loves most of all. With Jeanne's milky skin delicately nuanced by the soft light of a sun forbidden to rise.

"My little Jeanne, you're so beautiful as a bride!"

Eva feels her throat tighten. Now it's herself she's admiring in the cheval glass of her bedroom.

"Strange. It's as if I'm seeing myself."

Jeanne does not reply.

Eva sets to work. Her fingers fly over the canvas. As if they already know what Eva expects of them.

Jeanne does as she's told. Not moving, but not letting herself go either. Her entire being is fighting against the happiness the bridal gown should bring her. It is as if she were absent.
Eva suddenly has the feeling she's drawing a ghost. An invisible being. Only the gown and the headdress seem real. She no longer recognizes her sister. Her own flesh and blood is escaping from her. Jeanne is no more than a lifeless shape.
Behind her Eva still feels Henri's indecipherable, undeciphered gaze fixed on this singular scene; a gaze so intense that she must obey him, even if she does not understand what he requires of her.
She would like to ask Jeanne to look up, for suddenly she is cold and wants to seek the warmth of her sister's eyes. But she does not dare.
Jeanne's eyes are absent too. Departed to the land of melancholy. A melancholy that is insurmountable, indecipherable; in which there is no place for Eva, in which their pas de deux is impossible precisely because it requires the two of them in harmony, as at the time of their pastel duet, *The Favorite Plant*.
A mysterious threat is emanating from the picture. For the first time Jeanne is refusing herself to Eva.

Eva shudders.

If she had to give a name to the chill in her heart, would she call it a "premonition"?

"Eva, why? Why are you painting this portrait of me in your wedding dress?"

Eva gives a start. She gazes deep into the eyes of someone who seems to have woken from a distressing dream.

Her eyes remain fixed on her sister, the sister she loves so tenderly.

"I don't know," she replies. "But I have to."

* * *

Barely four years later, on May 6, 1883, Eva Gonzalès died of a blood clot to the brain aged thirty-six—only a few days after the death of her teacher Edouard Manet, and just after she had given birth to a son, Jean Raymond, whom Jeanne then raised as her own child.

Five years later, Jeanne married Henri Guérard, her sister's husband.

It is not known what dress she wore that day. The one in the picture?*

* Titled *A Bride*, the picture was shown at the Salon in Paris in 1885, not far from *The Favorite Plant*.

Eva Gonzalès (1847–1883)

1847	Eva Gonzalès is born in Paris on April 19, the daughter of the writer Emmanuel Gonzalès and his wife Marie Céline Ragut.
1866	She begins her training as a painter and draftswoman in the studio of Charles Chaplin and registers as a copyist in the Louvre.
1868	Chaplin cautions his friend Gonzalès against giving his daughter her own studio on the grounds that Eva should marry first.
1869	Alfred Stevens introduces the Gonzalès family to Edouard Manet. Eva becomes one of his pupils and often sits for him as well. Manet's remarks on Gonzalès's looks and talent lead to tensions with Berthe Morisot, who is eight years her senior.
1870	When Gonzalès exhibits three works at the Salon de Paris for the first time, Chaplin tells Eva's father he should rent a studio for her after all. Manet's *Portrait of Eva Gonzalès* is rejected by critics, Gonzalès's own painting *Enfant de Troupe* is purchased by the French state.
1872	Emile Zola praises Gonzalès's work *Indolence* on show at the Salon and her painting *Teatime* on show at the World Exposition in Lyon is commended as "honorable."
1873	After the jury turns down her submissions to the Salon, Gonzalès for the first and only time exhibits her works at the Salon des Réfusés.

1874 The Salon jury rejects *A Loge in the Théâtre des Italiens*, but accepts her pastel drawing *The Pink Morning*. Gonzalès then exhibits *A Loge* at the Salon triennial in Ghent. The critics are delighted, some of them even going so far as to claim that she has outstripped Manet in some respects.

1879 Gonzalès marries the painter and engraver Henri Guérard. Having been turned down in 1874, *A Loge in the Théâtre des Italiens* is now admitted to the Salon after all.

1880 The pastel drawing *The Maid of Honor* meets with universal praise in the press.

1883 Gonzalès dies of an embolism on May 6, shortly after the birth of her son Jean and just one week after Manet.

1885 The first retrospective held on the premises of the magazine *La Vie Moderne* in Paris is organized by Henri Guérard, Emmanuel Gonzalès, and Léon Leenhoff and brings together more than eighty different works. With the assistance of the gallery owner Durand-Ruel, the auction house Drouot is able to sell a number of her pastels, watercolors, and paintings. *On the Threshold* and *The Pink Morning* are purchased by the French state.

1889, 1900 Both these World Expositions in Paris include works by Gonzalès.

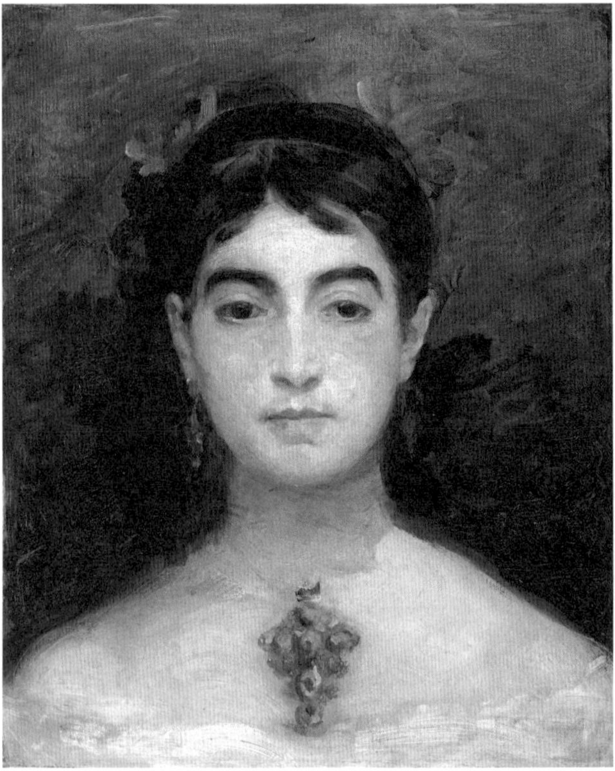

Marie Bracquemond, *Self-Portrait,* ca. 1870

Annette Pehnt

Where White Leaps into Purple

Sèvres, Sunday evening, 1880

Line versus color versus line versus color. The quarrel is not mine, for I already know how it will go, but Bracquemond forces me to take part so as to add luster to his own performance. Although only in front of an audience, of course. I can hear him even in the kitchen, where Emma and I are checking the roast, dipping our heads into the rosemary-scented steam, the heat hitting me in the face, and that is how I want to remain, having no wish to return to the table where they are talking and arguing.

Degas is there too, he looks at me across the table, and his looks go further than they should as I well know and he knows too. Only Bracquemond is oblivious, because he has to argue, has to come to the line's defense, knowing full well that his own lines are liable to become ropes in which he will become entangled and unable to extricate himself again.

While I am tending the roast, Emma fetches the sauciere, actually we're ready to eat now, Madame, she says, and then looks at me. I am forever in another's gaze, there is hardly a moment in which not a single eye is fixed on me, yet I should be glad of it, for what would I be if no one noticed me at all.

Emma wants us to take in the roast while it is still hot, and watches every move I make, as I become increasingly erratic, wiping the handles on the stove for the umpteenth time, nudging the firewood together with my foot—that loose pile of chocolate-brown chunks of wood, their sawn faces as yellowy-white as curdled milk. I hear him very clearly without needing to go in, I know what he is saying, and know that Degas will try to placate him, and that Manet will infuriate him all over again, and I know Louise's silent and proud face, so like my own, she is merely a witness and does not become involved, nor does she need to, because she understands nothing of all this and doesn't want to either.

I understand it very well and both want to and don't want to.

I have no strength for the fight Félix has started, every meal is a fight, a battle—among friends, of course. Once everyone has arrived—Degas invariably the first, Manet quite often late, the Sisleys only occasionally—Félix raises his glass and opens the evening with a toast.

To art, he cries, but to which art, and he laughs defiantly, eagerly awaiting the first riposte. It starts out as a game, they play and refill their glasses and spoon up the

cream of tomato soup that Emma has brought in, Louise looks across the table at me, raising her eyebrows as if to say, so when will it start?
Just be patient, it is about to start now, but first the little one has to go to bed. Emma, would you please put Pierre to bed, he can hardly keep his eyes open, he's so tired, isn't that so, Pierre? He protests, wants to stay with us, knows it is about art, in other words about everything, he wants to be a painter, too, in fact he already is one, look, Maman, look what I've painted, there are you and there is Papa, and there is the horse in the paddock behind the mill.
Plein air, that's dangerous, my child, if Papa knew you had been painting outside! But the little one can paint wherever he likes, his father is delighted and has built him a little easel and even refrains from scolding him when he splatters his shirt, look what happens when you mix yellow and red, do you see?
If I risk it, though, I can be sure of a reprimand, perhaps not immediately, but the Sunday following for sure, when the guests have arrived, the soup has been supped, the little one has at last fallen asleep, that is my moment of reckoning.
Yet I still carry the things out into the garden, there where the wasps hover above the lilac, or across the lawn to the marguerites and asters, where white leaps into purple and the sunlight is dappled by the birch

twigs and it is difficult to keep one's eyes open with all that light and all those colors swirling through the afternoon, while he is at the factory and Emma is in her room and Louise is in the darkened salon. Only Pierre is with me, watching me, looking at me, I must talk to him, but I can do that without thinking, I talk to him in a friendly way, kick his ball to him, or help him to set up his little easel next to my big one, and at the same time look at the colors and see no lines no matter how hard I stare: It is all light and sun so strong, I have to narrow my eyes and laugh quietly to myself.

Why are you laughing, Maman, asks Pierre, and I tell him it is because today is such a beautiful day.

Sometimes I lose track of time and Bracquemond comes home before I have removed the evidence, appearing suddenly at my side. I have nothing to fear as yet, there is no one here, so there will be no fight, he looks at the canvas and at the flower beds pulsating with sunlight, and places his hand on my neck, where I have always liked to be touched. He squeezes the skin on my neck, and pulls me towards him and I lean against him, and he calls me his water nymph, although there is no water here, but I know what he means. I am floating on this summer evening as if in light-spangled water, and he sees it in my picture and in my face. Perhaps it would be better if we stopped entertaining guests, then it could stay this way with my afternoons in the garden, in the water, he has understood, and it could stay this way, if we were alone together.

He then bends down to talk to Pierre and laughs with pride, not that he cares what Pierre has produced, he always praises him and lifts him up in the air, one day, my little one, you will be a painter just like your Daddy.

In which case he will need a sizable inheritance, I cut in, just to rib him, my passionate artist-husband who earns his bread with his pots. I thought I could do that, rib him, I mean, that in the pulsating light of summer we could tease each other gently before I take Pierre back inside and check on the preparations for supper, because although Emma is reliable, she does need a few words and looks of encouragement—which of us does not?

But the summer light is no help at all, nor Pierre's narrow face, streaked with paint, and his shouts as he runs across the lawn in pursuit of the cat, her swollen belly already hanging down like a bag full of shopping, so heavy that Pierre comes very close to catching her.

Inheritance—why? says Bracquemond, his voice now darker than before.

Do you really believe our son could not earn his own money, he says gloomily, and before I can explain what I meant—it was said in fun, a witty remark—he says, or do you consider me a poor example for him.

No no, I say, what nonsense, my love, what are you talking about, and then he interrupts me again.

These are words I do not want to hear, not from you, now I know what you really think of me, you think I do not earn enough, am not successful enough—but what is it you want? Tell me what you want and I will buy it for you.

Looking defiant with his hands on his hips, he takes a step towards me. I bend over my painting things and start packing up hastily, it would be best to say nothing and remain quiet at least until he leaves off and goes into the house and Emma brings him a glass of white wine.

Papa, calls Pierre from behind the roses, come here and look at the cat, she's as fat as my ball! But Bracquemond is not listening and cannot leave off me. He grabs me by the neck, but this time differently, and pulls me up and turns me round to face him, and he is so strong that I do not even try to wrest myself free of his hands.

What shall I buy you, he asks, in a soft, menacing voice.

You know I want for nothing, I mumble, shall we go inside

What do others have that you do not have.

I have everything I need, I whisper, which is not true, for it occurs to me instantly what I need, but it is nothing he could buy me, he would have to let me go.

You want to paint, he says, I'll buy you what you need, I'll bring you paints and canvas, large canvases, bigger and bigger, for you really are insatiable. And what else.

Had he asked the way he used to, softly, but still with this bear-like strength known to me only from Ingres, then I could have answered him. But not even the answer would have helped. He knows the answer, he must surely know it from what happened before, he knows what I want.
I have a hand and an eye, I have the knowledge, I had teachers too and all of this I carry within me, but I have no soil in which all this can grow.
So what else do you want.
It is pointless standing in front of each other like this, he knows it, we both know it. What we have to do now is detach our gazes from each other, turn away and gently slip off the noose that such moments inevitably place around us. Perhaps Emma will call me in a minute, or Pierre will run to me screaming because the cat has scratched his arm in order to teach him that she is not to be treated like a toy, and certainly not with a belly like this.
But no one comes and we stay rooted to the spot for a while and it seems to me that dusk is falling as if time were speeding past us, with only us left behind, frozen in this duel of ours.
And then it is over again, it always ends at some point and sometimes he even apologizes, even if only at night, when I can no longer see his face. He pulls me towards him, his bushy beard stroking my neck and face, he

knows that I will want to remain on my side of the bed after such a duel, but this makes him all the more eager to possess me. He has only to apologize and my defiance disintegrates, my bitter solitude subsides, I let him have his way and let him say sorry.

My water-nymph, my beauty, you know how much I want you, you shall have everything you need, I want to take care of you, I want you to be happy.

And I am almost proud to have this powerful man—Bracquemond, as I still call him—desire me so.

He then lies down on top of me, although he is very heavy, his body solid and strongly built, there is no hesitation, I hold my breath, but I like it, too, it is so forceful and overpowering, then he lowers himself onto me and cups my face in his hands, the best moment of all.

I often think of Degas at such moments, in so many ways the exact opposite, although he, too, is given to mockery, Manet says he lacks all naturalness, that he is incapable of loving a woman. But he is wrong about that, for Degas has never looked at him the way he looks at me with those mischievous, mocking eyes of his, at the same time saying something incredibly clever and sweeping his soft brown hair off his brow in a gesture that would be equally becoming in a girl.

When I was first married, Degas told me I deserved to have a lover if only on account of my eyebrows, and although his remark was utterly lacking in propriety and made me blush deeply, I was able to return his gaze so as not to forget that look.

Bracquemond says Degas never stayed long in the Café Guerbois, certainly not on Thursdays when everyone else was there and the arguments were flying back and forth like projectiles, he would stop by only for a while and quarrel with everyone briefly before rushing off with his pointed nose held high in the air. It is indeed true that Degas's nose turns up slightly at the end, although there is nothing stuck-up about it, on the contrary it lends him a somewhat streamlined quality, the sleek skittishness of a deer scenting the air.

Bracquemond thinks highly of Degas, despite making fun of him, but in the Café Guerbois it is actually de rigueur to ridicule him, which is why Bracquemond believes I would not have been able to stand it there, no one would have wanted to hear my conciliatory murmurings and doubtless I would not have survived it in any case—all that no-holds-barred quarreling, and quite rightly, too.

For the issues were indeed weighty ones.

I did not want to be there in any case, at least not at the table, but perhaps at the rear of the saloon, where no one would have seen me, but I would still have been able to hear something of their altercations, which after all—as long as Bracquemond was not the only one talking, which he certainly was not, there being far too many other intelligent minds present who were more than a match for him—concerned questions that were of interest to me, too. I would have done no more than listen, just like Monet, whom Bracquemond described as a taciturn guest and who never once opened his mouth, nor did he often have questions put to him, for Manet and Degas were not especially interested in landscapes, he simply wanted to be there, knowing that everyone in the group was looking only for truthfulness.

I would have listened and enjoyed a few sips of wine and enjoyed the truthfulness, too, flashes of which might have become visible in the men's crosstalk, and no one would have noticed me, least of all Bracquemond, who would have felt like one caught in the act and would have shooed me off back home, only Degas would have turned round to me from time to time and nodded at me almost imperceptibly.

But Pierre had already been born by then, a very restless child, always hungry, I was not very good at looking after him, since I had no strength and no milk either. Louise stood by me, and I'm not sure whether I would have got back on my feet without her, but she was often a thorn in my side as well, saying what I myself thought, but in such a way that it hurt me.

Bracquemond was a poor father, who instead of supporting me preferred to squander what little money he had with his buddies in the café, she said, and he hardly ever

looked at the child, and he ought to see that I was not in good health.
Yes, but what was he supposed to do.
I defended him to Louise, although her accusations were my own, and I cannot imagine what would have happened without her, so often did she carry Pierre through the apartment in the Rue de l'Université, he slept better in her arms than in mine. She organized our meals for us when I could not get up, and in winter she even fetched firewood for us because we could not afford servants. One could even say that Louise was my servant during that period, although she was stronger and better than I was, my feisty little sister, she is still so lovely, I shall paint her.
In the Auvergne, when Aunt Julienne told us fairytales on a winter evening, we would snuggle up together in front of the fire, and although she was smaller than me it was she who held my hand and who took me to the toilet out in the courtyard in case there were wolves waiting to get me. It was not right of me to use her as a servant, but I had no choice. Every other day, she made me a beef tea so strong it would have brought the dead back to life, and she drove out my bouts of fever with poultices. Perhaps she is my guardian angel, too. She certainly helps me when I want to go to church on Sundays and Bracquemond scoffs at me, laughing out loud at my piety, he would prefer to keep me inside the house

and the child even more so, but Pierre is already ten and old enough not to let himself be pushed around, he wants to go to Mass, too, and Louise escorts us out of the house with such gracious determination that Bracquemond dares not stand in our way. Nor would he ever raise a hand against us, his violence is the violence of words, not deeds, and the force he is unable to channel into his brushwork is channeled into his speech.

Louise would not be placated when we moved to the country, because of you, said Bracquemond, so that the clean air will restore you to health, but that was not enough for Louise.

He dumps you out here in the boondocks and thinks that is all he has to do, and who spends every Thursday living it up in Paris, says Louise

I cannot possibly do without Louise, but I do sometimes wonder what it would be like without her. She is always there. Perhaps she wants me to send Bracquemond away so that she can have him, because she never got anyone else.

That is how it was right at the start, when he was courting me. He would not give up. Maman instantly suspected the worst.

I was sitting in the Louvre working on Rembrandt, Maman and Louise were loitering in the background so as not to disturb me, because they knew how hard I have to concentrate when I am working. Whenever an admirer stopped and tried to chat with me, however, they would immediately come forward and take such a lively part in the conversation that the admirer soon tired of it and began beating a polite and friendly retreat. We would then put our heads together and giggle and Louise, who has a gift for mimicry, would imitate the gentleman so well that soon we would be beside ourselves with laughter, even Maman let down her guard, and our frolicsome threesome again attracted so much attention that the next one would begin by raising his eyebrows in a well-meaning sort of way. This one is for you, I would whisper to Louise, who would instantly laugh him off, knowing only too well that all the gentlemen who came by were interested in me alone, and she didn't even seem to resent it either.

You Spaniard, she sometimes said to me, you black beauty you, I would choose you too if I were a man.

Bracquemond was not to be deterred, however. He came to us day after day, watched me working, and then allowed his eyes to roam, from Rembrandt to my copy, to my hands, to my face, until I flushed. He had a certain strength which I found disconcerting, even without knowing him. Montrosier, who on one occasion happened to come by, introduced us to each other, and Bracquemond made a number of remarks to show me how much he knew about art, I saw through his ploy, but found it flattering nonetheless.

He endured Maman's and Louise's interjections by laughing sardonically or by making a barbed reply which was often enough to silence even Maman. Yet he was not impolite, he chatted amiably to Louise about Etampes and to Maman about the weather and the dampness of the air in the Louvre. Louise got so close to him it was as if she wanted to smell him, which was certainly not seemly and is not at all typical of her, she wanted him to look at her, though, and eventually he did so, cocking his head on one side and chatting, but chatting about art with me alone. His voice was loud and I could always hear him, even when he was talking to someone in the next room.

I liked to have him near me, I knew he had chosen me and it would not be long before I was his, a thought which pleased me.

When he asked Maman for my hand, she was scarcely able to turn him down, I was twenty-nine, an age at which marriage had long been on the cards.

We have every reason to be happy, said Maman, and yet. And then burst into tears, one of her usual fits of crying, but this one was more intense and lasted much longer than did most, because she could see my unhappiness coming, marry this man, she sobbed, and you will be condemning yourself to misery.

He is an artist, I told her proudly, and artists know how to make women happy.

He is coarse, sobbed Maman, he is not made of the same stuff as you are. Take any man you like, an artist, too, if you will, but not him.
I saw very well the stuff that Bracquemond was made of, and that was what I wanted, I wanted that solidity, that coarseness, and thought that if I grazed myself on it, then I would become wiser and stronger.
I now have lots of grazes and even several cuts. The scars are too innumerable to count. And I have become wiser, too.
But I may not show them to Maman, nor even to Louise, who is so often witness to their making. Sometimes she takes me to one side the morning after and says why do you allow yourself to be treated like that. Why do you let him behave like that, this blockhead.
But he always apologizes, I say, apologetically.
And that really is how it is. And what would I be without him. At least I still have him, which is more than Maman can say. She is now growing old without a husband and her face is becoming gaunter and more pinched with every year that passes, which does not suit her at all, so that is what she gets for all that freedom and roaming around. She takes pride in the fact that she did not allow her captain to boss her around and then he was dead and the next one was not much better and had to learn his lesson, and if she didn't like it then she simply moved on. Yet she has not preserved her free spirit,

but instead has shed all her gentleness, all her softness, and has become a block of wood, almost as hard and angular as my Bracquemond.
And in the night she lies alone in her old body, with no one to pull her towards him or who knows the scars on her body, every single one of them, and who caresses them, as only he who made them can do best.

The meat sweltering in the roasting tin. The bubbles of boiling fat on the crust burst almost soundlessly, tiny detonations, I hold my hand over it so that I can feel the hot fat stinging the palm of my hand. And then lift the sizzling-hot meat onto a silver trencher. Emma ties on her apron and using a linen dishtowel gives the big carving knife one last wipe, we cannot start carving though, because Bracquemond insists on doing that himself.
The scent of rosemary, almost bitter, causes us to linger at the stove for a moment, until Emma nods to me, as if it were her job to give orders, and holding the trencher in both hands pushes open the door to the dining room. I take off my apron and follow her slowly.
When I enter the room, Bracquemond is standing at the head of the table, his glass raised ready to make a toast, in front of him the roast on the gleaming trencher. All eyes are trained on him, only Degas turns to look at me. Bracquemond clears his throat, and I know what he is about to say.

I take my place beside him and remove the wine from his hand. I look round at the guests, at Degas, Manet, Sisley. It is completely silent.
This will be my year, I say quietly, and raise my glass.

Marie Bracquemond (1840–1916)

1840 Marie is born on December 1 in Argentan in Brittany, the daughter of the sea captain Théodore Quivoron and his wife Aline Pasquiou. She grows up under difficult circumstances. Following the death of her father, Marie and her mother embark on what is to be a nomadic existence.

1854 Move to Etampes, 50 km south of Paris. Marie has drawing lessons with the painter Auguste Vassort and begins painting watercolor landscapes. She meets Jean Auguste Dominique Ingres and has lessons with his pupils, Désiré François Laugée and Emile Signol. First official commissions. Marie becomes the breadwinner for her mother and sister Louise.

1859 Her works are exhibited at the Salon de Paris, in which she will henceforth be a regular participant.

1866 She meets the artist and engraver Félix Bracquemond in the Louvre and they marry in 1869.

1870 Birth of her only child, Pierre

1872 Félix is put in charge of the Auteuil branch of the Haviland porcelain factory of Limoges. Marie continues to exhibit her works at the Salon, but becomes increasingly involved in her husband's activities in the workshop in Auteuil.

1876 At an exhibition of the Union centrale des arts appliqués à l'industrie in Paris, Bracquemond exhibits various porcelain vessels and painted plaques as well as the faience plaque *The Muses of the Arts* which Haviland will later display at the World Exposition of 1878 as an example of decorative ceramics.

1877 The art critic Philippe Burty counts Marie Bracquemond as one of "the most intelligent pupils to come out of the Ingres workshop."

1879, 1880 At the invitation of Edgar Degas, Bracquemond exhibits her works together with those of the other Impressionists.

1881 Exhibits in London

1886 Bracquemond contributes six works to the last Impressionist exhibition. She organizes soirées to which Edgar Degas, Edouard Manet, Henri Fantin-Latour, Paul Gauguin, and Auguste Rodin are invited.

1890 Marie takes part in an exhibition at the Galerie Durand-Ruel in Paris. At the urging of her husband Félix, Marie gradually abandons painting altogether.

1916 After living for a long time as a recluse, Marie dies in Sèvres on January 17.

1919 The first retrospective at the Galerie Bernheim-Jeune in Paris comprises 161 exhibits, including ninety paintings, thirty-four watercolors, and nine etchings—but no ceramics. The City of Paris buys the painting called *The Afternoon Tea*.

Authors´ Biographies

Born in Antwerp in 1946, **Diane Broeckhoven** is now back in her native city after thirty years in the Netherlands. She has published some twenty books for young people, many of which have won important literary prizes. *De buitenkant van Meneer Jules* (2005), her second book for adult readers, was a bestseller in Germany. Her third novel *Reiskoorts* was published in 2006.

Noëlle Châtelet was born in 1944 and lives in Paris. Besides having been a lecturer in Communications Science, she was head of the Institut Français in Florence from 1989 to 1991, co-president of the Maison des écrivains in Paris, and in 2003 was appointed vice president and in 2007 honorary president of the Société des Gens de Lettres. She has published novels, short stories, and essays for which she has received innumerable prizes, including the Prix Goncourt de la nouvelle for her *Histoires de Bouches,* the Prix Anna de Noailles of the Académie française for *La dame en bleu,* and the Prix Renaudot des lycéens for *La dernière leçon.* Many of her books have been translated and some have been adapted for the stage or made into movies. Châtelet is also an actress and played in *Vera Baxter* by Marguerite Duras, in *La Banquière* by Francis Girod, and in the eleven-part TV series *Les Buddenbrook.*

Annette Pehnt was born in Cologne in 1967 and now lives with her family in Freiburg. She studied Celtic Studies, English, and German in Freiburg, Berkeley, California, and Galway, Ireland, and has a doctorate in Irish literature. Her works include the novels *Ich muß los* (2001), *Insel 34* (2003), *Haus der Schildkröten* (2006) and *Mobbing* (2007), two children's books *Rabea und Marili* (2006) and *Annika und die geheimnisvollen Freunde* (2007), and a collection of prose called *Herr Jakobi und die Dinge des Lebens* (2005).

Born in 1961, **Alissa Walser** is the youngest daughter of German writer Martin Walser and lives in Frankfurt am Main. From 1981 to 1986 she studied painting in New York and Vienna. Her short story *Geschenkt* won her the Ingeborg Bachmann Prize 1992, and she was awarded the Bettina von Arnim Prize that same year. Her first collection of short stories *Dies ist nicht meine ganze Geschichte* was published in 1994 and was followed in 2000 by another called *Die kleinere Hälfte der Welt.* Besides writing works of her own, Walser also works as a translator from English into German.

The anthology **Painting in a Man's World**
is published on the occasion of the exhibition
Women Impressionists – Morisot, Cassatt, Gonzalès, Bracquemond
Schirn Kunsthalle, Frankfurt
February 22 to June 1, 2008
Fine Arts Museums of San Francisco
June 21 to September 21, 2008

Editor: Ingrid Pfeiffer
Conception and editing: Eike Barbara Dürrfeld, Kathrin Luz, Neumann Luz (Cologne)
Copyediting: Melanie Newton
Translations: Sherry Marx (Broeckhoven), Burton Pike (Walser), Bronwen Saunders (Pehnt), John Tittensor (Châtelet)
Graphic design: Simone Zeeb, Gabriele Sabolewski
Typeface: Relay, FF Eureka
Paper: Munken Print White, 115 g
Binder: IDUPA, Schübelin GmbH, Owen
Reproductions: Dr. Cantz'sche Druckerei, Ostfildern
Printed by Offizin Chr. Scheufele, Stuttgart

Published by
Hatje Cantz Verlag
Zeppelinstraße 32
73760 Ostfildern
Tel. +49 711 4405-200
Fax +49 711 4405-220
www.hatjecantz.com

ISBN 978-3-7757-2077-9
German edition: ISBN 978-3-7757-2076-2

Printed in Germany

Cover illustration: Eva Gonzalès, *The Chignon,* 1865–70 (detail), oil on canvas, 51 x 40, private collection

p. 14: Berthe Morisot, *Self-Portrait,* 1885, oil on canvas, 61 x 50 cm, Musée Marmottan, Paris; © The Bridgeman Art Library Nationality

p. 34: Mary Cassatt, *Self-Portrait,* 1878, gouache on paper, 60,1 x 41,2 cm, The Metropolitan Museum of Art, New York. Bequest of Edith H. Proskauer, 1975; © 2007 Image copyright / Art Resource / Scala, Florence

p. 54: Edouard Manet, *Portrait of Eva Gonzalès,* 1870, oil on canvas, 191 x 133 cm, National Gallery, London; © The Bridgeman Art Library Nationality

p. 72: Marie Bracquemond, *Self-Portrait,* ca. 1870, oil on canvas, 45 x 38 cm, private collection; photo: Martine Beck Coppola

Biographies: Sylvia Metz

Acknowledgements
Susanne Bader, Graf & Graf
Kristina Beseler, Piper Verlag
Gudrun Fähndrich, Kiepenheuer & Witsch
Christina Knorr, Beck Verlag
Regina Steinicke, Rowohlt Verlage

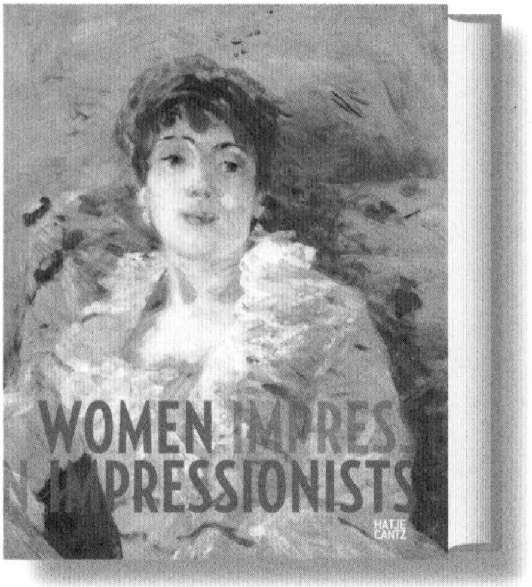

Impressionism is a woman!

Women Impressionists

Berthe Morisot, Mary Cassatt,
Eva Gonzalès, Marie Bracquemond

C. 400 pp., c. 350 ills.,
hardcover
C. $60.00
ISBN 978-3-7757-2079-3
February 2008

The first publication on the most important women Impressionists with many unfamiliar and surprising images, waiting to be discovered by both fans of and newcomers to Impressionism.

Hatje Cantz Verlag, Germany
www.hatjecantz.com

HATJE
CANTZ